Apart from Our Own

Own

The "Healers"

A. R. Fisher

Chapter 1

The newspaper was lying on the kitchen table. The headlines were of a house fire. I sat down and started reading the front page. Under the picture of the house was a small description. *A house in this small town was nearly engulfed by flames. Firefighters still do not know the cause of the fire. Two boys by the names of Petey and Danny only suffered minor burns.*

I dropped the paper and ran to Petey's house.

φ φ φ

There were fire trucks that had blocked off the road, and the ambulances were huddled in the center of the mob. As I walked through the crowd I checked in the back of each ambulance and still didn't find Petey. My heart was now pounding out of my chest, and every possible bad thought of what could have happened to Petey was now running through my head. I found Danny and asked him where Petey was. He looked at me with sad eyes then looked toward the house. Everything around me became a blur. The sirens blended together and my body became stiff.

"Where's Petey?" I managed to get out.

"He's getting fixed up," Danny said.

"What?" I asked coming out of my daze. Here I am thinking Petey was gone, and Danny is saying he's not?

"He's over there."

I followed where Danny was pointing and saw Petey getting wrapped up by a lady in a blue uniform. I ran over to him and impatiently waited for a hug.

"Are you okay?" I asked while hugging him.

"I think so," he said getting up. The lady nurse put a brown blanket around his shoulders. "Thanks."

He looked at me then opened the blanket up for another hug. I ignored his want for a hug and looked at him instead. He didn't look too different, but my stomach flipped when I saw the few small burn marks on his cheek and neck.

"Come here," he said. "I desperately need a hug."

I gladly walked into his arms again and held him tight. I heard him start to get worked up. "Sshh, sshh, sshhh. You and Danny will figure out something. It will all be okay."

I could feel that the arm around my shoulder had a fair amount of gauze pads on it. I gently backed out of his hug. "Is it bad?"

"It's the start of a second degree burn. It hurts right now, but I'll be okay. I was trying to save my pictures."

I'm usually really good with words in trying times, but I just can't think of anything to say except *I'm sorry.* "I should really be saying something, but I just don't know what to say Petey."

"I know," he said.

He slowly turned and walked toward the house. I stood in my spot and watched him. I felt Danny come over to me, but didn't look in his direction.

"He was lucky," Danny said.

"What do you mean?" I asked looking at Danny.

"I mean he almost didn't make it out. Mom and dad were certainly watching out for us today."

"Did they ever tell you the start of the fire?" I asked.

"No, they didn't."

Chapter 2

I was sliding down a water slide into a white flash. The flash brought me into and underworld. It was a world under the water.

I slowly opened my eyes and looked to the dark ceiling.

"Already?" I said.

I didn't sleep the rest of the night because I was too anxious about telling Penny about the new world.

φ φ φ

"Penny."

"Moni? It's six in the morning on a Saturday."

"I know, I'm sorry, but I just saw a new world. I think."

"How? It's too soon."

"I don't know. It was my first vision. Maybe it's a false alarm. Will I see you later?"

"Yeah, but for right now, I'm going back to bed."

I smiled as I hung up the phone.

φ φ φ

Penny came over after dinner. We were sitting on my bed with my TV on mute.

"So tell me about this dream?" I told her about the water slide and the flash. "We will just research it like we did with the mirror world."

"What do you think this world will show us?"

"Maybe it will be an extension off our last adventure," she guessed.

"Petey won't like it if we have to go through that again. And neither will I." I looked down to the ground as I was twiddling my thumbs. "Can I ask what your reflection was?"

"You can ask, but I can't tell you. Maybe this world will show our memory so we don't have to tell." She almost sounded hopeful.

φ φ φ

I was sliding down a water slide into a bright white flash. The flash brought me into and underwater world, but I wasn't wet. I was as dry as if I was on land. I felt something come into connection with my mind and wanted to wake up but I couldn't. The connection became part of me as my memories were being sorted on a giant water screen. There was a memory that remained in the middle of the screen. I slowly came out of the dream.

Penny was right. This is just an extension off our last adventure.

Chapter 3

We told Petey what the new world might be.

"I don't think I'll be able to handle that again."

"It's not like we are going to relive it. I think it's going to show us something different," I said to Petey.

"Different how?" he asked.

"Well, it's a water world." I said opening my laptop. "What does water do?"

"Brings life?"

"Right, but it can also heal."

Penny smiled and I looked at Petey. "You up for it?"

"Petey, if you can get through your worst memory, then you can get through anything. Besides we can't split this group up. It wouldn't feel right with three people. We need that number four," Penny said.

"If this world can heal my memory then I'm all for it," he said.

I felt a smile come across my face. "That's my boy."

After the conversation about the new world we went off on our talks that we had before the worlds came into our lives. It was a magical day and I felt complete, well almost.

My brother let Penny spend the night. We were in my room, her on the floor and me in my bed. "I should get a day bed in here so you don't have to be on the floor anymore."

"Make that soon. The floor doesn't exactly contour to your body."

It was nighttime and the beach was closed. I was only spring too, so the fence was locked. I put my hand on one half of the locked gate and pushed forward. The opening became big enough for me to squeeze through. Petey, Mickey and Penny were following me. I was forced to stop by a glow of light in the water and walked closer to it. My foot hit the water and I fell into a flash.

I opened my eyes and Penny was next to me.

"Anything new?"

"It's in the water at the water park."

"That's kind of cool. When do we leave?" she asked.

"When we want," I said lying back down.

"We will leave in the morning. I am texting Mickey and Petey now. They will wake up to the message."

"Okay," I said looking at my digital clock on my nightstand. It was only 1 am.

φ φ φ

Morning came all to fast. I was still facing the wall, but I could feel a body behind me. I slowly turned my head. Penny was still asleep. I turned to my back and looked at the ceiling, then at her. I slowly sat up and gently took her arm off me. I heard a knock on the door as I was making my way to the bottom of the bed.

"I have to work," Ryan said now standing in the doorway. "Will you be home?"

"Actually, there is another world. We are leaving tonight."

"Be careful."

"I will try."

He walked to me and brought me in for a hug. I put my head against his shoulder and put my arms around his waist. "Come back to me."

"I will," I said. I know I can't make any promises about coming home. Not with these worlds.

"Love you," he said releasing the hug.

"I'll see you for dinner," I said as a tear dripped onto my cheek.

"Yes you will," he said wiping the tear away. He kissed my forehead and slowly closed the door behind him as he left.

"Are you scared?"

I turned to Penny with a little jump.

"I'm scared about going to the world. Nervous about not making it back home. Ryan is all I have, and I am all he has."

"I will make sure you come back. Even if it kills me," she said. She got up from my bed and came over to me. She put her hand on my shoulder. "We are all in this together. I won't let anything happen to you."

Chapter 4

We had told the parents and siblings about the worlds when we returned from The Machine world. I wish there was some way they could stop us, but they can't. They all told us the same thing. *Be careful.*

We met up at Mickey's house around dinnertime, with our parents and siblings. They have told us that when we are not home, they have learned to cope with each other. They stay together until we come home.

"It's time to go," I say standing up from the table.

The house became quiet and everyone stood up. They slowly went to their parents or siblings. I had said goodbye to Ryan before.

"Are we ready?" Penny asked.

"Let's get this over with," I said turning to the door. As I took a step toward the door and hand touched my shoulder. It was Penny's mom.

"Please be careful."

"We will do the best we can," I told her. She hugged me then lightly pushed me to the door.

"Fearless leader," Penny's mom said.

I wouldn't say fearless.

We got to the sidewalk and refused to look back even though we wanted to.

"The next world is in the water." I said.

"Won't the water be cold, and wet? Cold and wet are not a good combination?" Penny said.

"We won't get wet, but it will be cold."

"Moni, this is crazy," Mickey said.

"Not as crazy as the machines. And we didn't know what were getting ourselves into then. At least now, we know what we are walking into."

"She's right. We have no choice," Petey said agreeing with me. I looked at him a little surprised. Him and I agree on very little.

We get to the locked fence from my dream. It felt like a de ja vu. I lifted my right hand and pushed one side of the fence forward. I squeezed through, and so did the rest of the gang. The four of us had our flashlights on and pointed down to the pavement path in front of us. I was feeling really tired as we walked up a hill to the water slides.

I didn't realize I was on my knees until I felt a hand on my shoulder.

"Moni, what do you see?"

I saw the pavement beneath my feet quickly being covered by a white line of light. It led me to a light blue glow in the water.

φ φ φ

"Moni," I heard Penny say.

"Moni, can you hear us?" Petey asked.

I slowly opened my eyes. "Yeah, I can hear you."

Petey smiled and lightly touched my cheek. "Can you sit up?"

"Yeah." I slowly sat up with Petey's hand behind my back.

"What did you see?" Mickey asked.

"I saw the way to get into the underworld."

The three of them helped me up and we started making our way to the slide from my vision. I looked down and saw the white line, but I think I was the only one that could see it.

We got to the slide, and I saw the same blue glow in the water.

"I don't see anything," Petey said.

"Neither do I," Mickey and Penny said at the same time.

I sat down and looked at the light only I could see. "I don't know."

I hung my head low and felt a hand on my arm. I looked up and Penny was looking towards the water. I could hear the water starting to bubble.

"Let's go," I said standing up. I headed towards the water, and then felt someone take hold of my hand.

"This can't be the only way," Penny said.

"Haven't you guys learned to trust my visions? It won't be open for much longer. You were hesitant on the other worlds too."

"This is different," Petey said coming up next to me as we stand on the shoreline.

"Different how?" I asked.

"I don't want to see the car crash again," he said.

"This world will take the pain again. We have to go," I said letting go of Penny's hand leaving them to look at each other.

I stood at the bottom of the slide with Mickey, as Petey and Penny came over. "This slide is the only way the portal will take you."

The wind started to kick up so I had to yell to make sure my friends heard me. *There is no backing out now.*

Penny went up first, then Mickey. Petey signaled for me to go next, but I didn't go up.

"You go first," I yelled.

"Not a chance. You first," he said. He grabbed both of the slide's railings on either side blocking me in. I had no choice but to go before him.

I reach the top as Mickey is sliding down and see the portal has taken him. The portal started blinking and I get a jolt of anxiety. I didn't know if it would take me, let alone take Petey who is behind me. I have gotten settled on the slide and felt Petey behind me.

"I'll see you soon," he said into my ear and gave me a gentle push. I turn to my stomach as I am sliding down to get one more glace at Petey. I close my eyes when I feel the cold water and pray the portal takes him and me. I was turned onto my back, not on my own terms, and stayed awake while in the portal. A little while later I felt the pull of the portal stop and gravity take over. I could see the ground fastly approaching and attempted to land on my feet.

Chapter 5

I looked around and was alone. I was in a gray room with freaky looking floors. There was a water pattern pretty much everywhere. The only window I could see was a few feet away on what looked like a door. I saw a tall, lanky figure pass and a little human figure behind it. The human figure stopped. I could only see the shadow until the figure came closer to the window. It was Penny. She waved then lifted one finger. She mouthed *one sec* and turned to the lanky creature next to her. The lanky creature came back to the window. Once the door open the creature guided Penny through the door with its hand. The creature's hand looked like he was just stretched out. All of its limbs are three times the length of mine, fingers and skull included.

"What is that?" I asked her.

"My healer."

"What?"

Penny helped me up. "You have one too."

The healer followed us out of the room. It was a strange place. It was big and very empty.

"Where is everyone?" I whispered to Penny as we walked.

"They will show you. Be patient."

The healer led the way to I don't know where. The walk feels like forever. We turned a corner and the biggest room I had ever seen made me feel smaller then normal. In the far corner of the room I could easily see a water TV. I thought the TV my neighbor has is big. I would like to see them fit this in their living room. As we walked closer to the TV I looked down at my feet. The floor looked like it was made of water. I took the next step then felt the bottom of my shoe. It was dry. *This place is weird.* I looked up from my shoes and could see Mickey and Petey. They were seated in metal chairs, I guess waiting for us. The healer sat Penny down and left me standing. A shadow came up behind me before I could turn around. My heart started to race when it touched me with its hand. He gently pushed me toward the only chair still available. As soon as I sat down I felt metal bands wrap around my ankles. My healer lifted my little arms onto the armrest, then metal bands wrapped around my wrists. The healer then pushed my head back. When it took its hand away a metal band held my head in place. When the four of us were braced in I could see that we each had a healer. They all looked the same. They were all tall, and all extremely thin. Their necks didn't look like they could hold up their abnormally shaped heads. They wore pants only, with a belt. The four healers each had a different symbol on the belt buckles.

"What is going to happen to us?" Penny asked with a shake in her voice.

"We are the Sayous. The healers. Each of you has an experienced a type of pain in your lifetime."

I heard the voice but didn't know which healer was speaking. None of their mouths were moving. This place keeps getting weirder and weirder.

"What does that mean?" Petey asked.

"After tonight, the pain will be no more."

"What's with the symbols on your pants?" I asked.

"We have been born to treat a type of pain. We grow into the symbol on our buckle."

The Sayous took a step closer to us all at the same time. I couldn't move anywhere and my breathing was becoming out of control.

"Moni. Moni. You need to relax," I heard Penny say.

"No I don't. This doesn't feel right."

I kept my eyes close, not wanting to see how close it is. I felt something happen. He must have touched the metal band around my head because I didn't feel anything new touch my skin. I could see my adventure from the mirror world. I could see mom, and dad in the kitchen with me in my high chair. Then I saw mom in her bedroom with the nurse and grandma and grandpa standing at the foot of the bed. I relived Dad coming up the stairs with the glass bottle in his hand. I heard a long beep as my adventure replayed in fast forward. All the pictures went black as mom stood in front of me.

"I was wrong," she said.

"Wrong about what?"

"About this. All of it. I just wanted to get you home."

"Mom wait."

"Fight it Moni. They will take this memory and you will never get it back. You will never remember me, or dad, or the pain our family went through. Fight to keep me alive Moni."

"I don't know how to fight it."

18

How could this be bad? We are getting rid of the memories because we don't need them anymore. That's what she told me. Then she said she was wrong? She wanted to get me home.

Mom is now gone, leaving me to fend in the dark, again. I open my eyes. I felt different. Drained. Not myself. I look over at Penny and she looks just as bad as I feel. The locks from our wrist and ankles have been opened. Our foreheads were free a little while after. The Sayous left in an orderly fashion. The four of us stood up not really knowing what just happened, or what to do about it. A random alien led us out from a nearby line up. We were taken back to the room I was in before I was brought out to the chairs. The door closed and was locked behind us.

"Something isn't right," I said.

"You're right, but what do we do?"

"Mine as well find a way to destroy this world too."

Penny smiled. "How we going to do that?"

"On accident," I said with a smile, followed by a wink.

φ φ φ

I was playing with the water on the floor. I kept pulling my finger out and feeling it. It was always dry. *That's still weird.* Every time something went by the window, I looked up. All the aliens looked the same.

"What was the big TV screen for?" Mickey asked.

"Don't know," I said. "And I hope were aren't here to find out."

The door finally opened. A Sayou came in and aggressively grabbed Mickey's arm.

"Wait," I yelled. "Take me first."

Mickey was dragged out of the room. He was trying to find something to grab onto. I ran for him but the door broke my path to him.

Chapter 6

"We have to do something!" I yelled. I turned around and looked at Penny and Petey. They hadn't moved from their spots.

"The door is locked on the outside," Petey said low without a sense of hope.

"Why did they take him anyway?" Penny asked now looking at the door.

"My mom told me that she was wrong. We still have the memory inside. It has been beaten and is now useless inside of us. I guess The Sayous are going to try to rid us of the pain. They are taking the memory and we won't be getting it back. I don't think we are getting healed at all."

"Maybe it's not memories they are healing?" Penny suggested.

"What do you mean?" I asked walking over and sitting down next to her.

"Petey has a burn on his arm (physical). You have a hard time letting go of that memory (mental). I have been on an emotional roller coaster lately (emotional). And Mickey. . .?"

"Maybe Mickey is spiritual?"

"He has been getting back into church," Petey chimed in. "He took that break for a little while when his dad passed away. That was when he had given up all hope of God protecting his family."

"But if he isn't getting healed, then, does that mean they are going to take away his spirit?" I asked looking at Petey, then to Penny.

"They can't do that. It will kill him," Petey said getting up and going over to the door.

We waited for a long while. Petey had started pacing, and Penny and I started getting antsy. The lights in our room went off. I stood up and reached my hand out for Penny's. Hers was right where I expected it to be. We walked toward the door, where Petey had stopped pacing. The three of us starred at the door as a click broke the silence. The door slid open and Mickey was drug passed us. The Sayou let go of Mickey's leg and let his hips drop to the floor. If I could've run over to Mickey at that instant I would have, but I felt numb. The Sayou walked passed us to the door, and locked it after closing it. I slowly went over to Mickey's hurt body and knelt down. Petey and Penny were behind me.

"Mickey," I said low trying to hold back tears. I touched his hair hoping to wake him up. I looked at his stomach to reassure myself that he was still breathing. He was. I looked to his face. "Please Mickey, open your eyes."

He slowly opened them.

"What happened?" Penny asked.

"I, I don't know. I can't remember. They strapped me in that chair again."

"How you feeling?" I asked.

He slowly sat up and crawled to the corner of the room away from us and lay on the floor. I looked back to Penny. I was now extremely worried about how this has effected Mickey in the long run. *Will he ever be the same?*

The lights in our room remained off, but the unknown light under the floor gave us more light then I hoped for. I'd much rather sit in the dark rather than to see where I am right now. I was sitting against the wall and managed to get Mickey to lie on my lap. The floor might look pretty, but it's cold. He was on his back facing me with closed eyes. I keep looking down at him just to keep my mind at ease that he is still alive.

"Do you know what I noticed when he opened his eyes before?"

"What?" Penny asked.

"He was empty. They took something. Whether it is his spirit or memory, they took something."

φ   φ   φ

I was still against the wall. Mickey had been out cold ever since he has been on my lap. He hasn't had anything to drink since we have gotten here. Actually none of us have.

I looked around the room and saw a fountain in the far corner that I didn't notice before. I gently nudged Penny's shoulder and pointed to the fountain. "Would you be able to get him some water?"

"How? I don't have a cup to bring it over in."

I went silent and looked down at my shirt's sleeve. "Rip my sleeve off."

"What?"

"Rip my sleeve off. It'll soak up the water enough to get it back across the room."

I got my legs into a different position while she was doing that. I gently lay Mickey's head on the floor and attempted to wake him up. Petey came over.

"Mickey, can I get you to drink some water?"

"I'm . . . not . . . thirsty," he managed to get out.

"I know you're tired, but I don't want you to be dehydrated on top of that. Let's get your strength back up so we can attempt to get out of here."

"I don't want any," he said pushing my water filled sleeve away again. He rolled into my body and went right back to sleep. His body instantly became relaxed and his breathing, slightly heavy.

I looked to Petey. "Maybe you can find a way to get his strength back up."

"I'll try. You and Penny should get some sleep. I'll take first watch."

"Are you sure Petey?" I asked.

"Yes I'm sure. Here," he said handing me his sweatshirt.

"Thanks."

"Wait," he said getting up. "Make the sweatshirt a blanket. I'll be your pillow."

I smiled and waited for him to get comfortable before I lay my head down.

φ φ φ

"It's your turn," the Sayou said.

No," I yelled pinning myself in the corner of the room. He grabbed my arm and led me out of the room. Another Sayou made sure the door closed behind us. "Why do you need the memory anyway?" The panic had set in. I was trying my hardest to break the grip of the Sayou, but my wrists were so small. His fingers could wrap around my arm five times, at least.

"Our survival. We heal because we must."

He stopped in front of the metal chairs. He wasn't doing anything. He just stood there causing my nerves to tighten. The suspense of what he was going to do to me would probably kill me before he did. He grabbed both of my arms and threw me into the chair before I even knew what happened. The straps held my wrists down. The Sayou held my legs down until the strap enclosed my ankles too. I kept my head forward so the band couldn't close me in. The Sayou put one finger on my head and pushed my head with no effort at all. I was straining my neck muscles so hard to not give in, but he was so much bigger than me. I couldn't do anything about it. I felt the metal band close around my head and finally gave up. I relaxed my neck and prepared for the worse. The Sayou was in front of me. He stood up straight and lifted his hand to the metal band. I knew he had touched the band when my mind started going a hundred miles an hour. He was sifting through my memories. He was looking for the one memory that I have hidden.

φ φ φ

The world around me was still dark when I woke up. I slowly sat up and looked down at Mickey. He was in the same position in which I left him. Penny was behind me with her head on her one arm. Her other arm was over me, lightly holding my hand. I looked at Petey, who had accidentally fallen asleep. His head was resting awkwardly on his right shoulder. I touched his arm and gently shook him.

"Petey," I whispered.

"What?" he answered back and lifted his head up.

"Your turn to lay down," I said starting to switch spots with him.

"How long have we been here?" he asked starting to move.

"I don't know. I left my watch at home."

When Petey got settled I lay my head against the wall and looked at the floor across the room. The water that formed the floor was beautiful in a way. I still find it a little odd that I can touch it without getting wet. It was reflecting whatever light was shining below it, creating a dancing light show on the four walls of our room.

I put my hand on Petey's shoulder and felt his hand grab mine. He took a deep breath and relaxed, his hand falling back to the floor. I looked down to Mickey and could kind of see the light from the floor reflecting off his forehead.

"Mickey," I said calmly moving Petey off my lap. I leaned forward and rolled Mickey to his back. "Mickey, what's wrong?"

"Moni? What is it?" Petey asked.

"I don't know."

Penny came over and helped to get Mickey onto my lap. I touched his forehead. He was warm.

"Get him some more water," I said calmly, pointing to the fountain.

Penny brought my sleeve back over full of water and I opened Mickey's mouth. "Drink Mickey."

"Come on buddy. You need to wake up," Petey said, finally showing some emotion.

Water droplets ran out the sides of Mickey's mouth, but he showed no movement. I dabbed his head with the cool rag, and finally got something. He moved his head and slowly opened his eyes.

"Hey," I said touching his cheek.

"Hi?"

"You okay?"

"Exhausted."

"Can you tell us what happened?"

Just then, the door opened and a Sayou walks in. The symbol on its belt tells me it's my turn.

Chapter 7

He came over to me and grabbed my arm. He yanked me up, letting Mickey's head hit the floor. I saw the water under his head splash, but his face did not get wet, and his hair still looked dry.

"Let go. You don't have to drag me. I will come."

The Sayou pulled me ahead of him and pushed me out the door. I wasn't able to catch a glimpse of any of my friends' faces. It might have been my last time seeing them. As we walked I looked back. I remember there being a huge window on the side of our room. I can see out of it, but as I walked I could not find any window. My dream was becoming real. The Sayou was behind me, with a hand on my back making sure I wasn't going anywhere except the place he wanted me to go. We were heading back to the chairs. When we got to the chairs we stopped and waited. He was thinking I would walk up the few steps into the chair myself, but I was hoping he would drop his hand from behind my back, so I could run back to my friends, my family. I looked up at him, and he pointed to the chairs, growing very impatient. I slowly walked toward the chairs, and the feeling of his hand left my back. This is as good of a chance as any. I turned and ran as fast as I could back to my friends. I slammed into the door, and banged until my fists hurt, then I banged some more. I looked down to the lock and it required more then just a turn of a knob. It required and thumb print. *Damn.*

The Sayou came around the corner, and I could hear Penny yell. "RUN!"

I ran away from the room with the chairs, and knew that if I were to be caught I would be in for a world of pain. This was his home. There will be no hiding because I'm sure he knows of them all. I'm not going to be able to get away. It was time to stand and fight. I rounded a corner, and saw nothing. It was darker the farther I looked. I stopped and didn't know where to go. I didn't know what was in the dark, but I think I would rather take my chances in the dark rather than wondering what he will do to me if he gets me. I walked slowly into the dark, watching my foot placement. I felt an open hallway on my right and felt around for the wall leading me to it. I felt a hand grab my wrist and jerk me down to the floor. Another hand covered my mouth.

"I'm here to help you. Please be quiet. I'm going to take my hand away from your mouth and you will not scream, or else we will both be found."

I nodded and he let me go. I felt him move around to the front of me and kneel down.

"Hi," he said.

"What are you doing?" I asked as he stood up.

"Sssh," he said leaning over to my level.

"You understand me?"

"Be quiet," he said more sternly. "I'll help you get back to that room."

"Who are you? You can't be a Sayou?" I asked getting up.

"I'm not."

"What are you?"

"We need to go."

He started heading farther into the corridor, and I did not hesitate to follow him.

"You know, your pretty stupid for running from a Sayou," he said stepping over something.

"Why?" I asked kicking whatever he just stepped over.

"Because he will get you back, and you'll be sorry."

That doesn't sound good.

"How many friends you have in that room?" he asked.

"Three. One has already been Drained, I guess is what I should call it?"

"How? I mean what kind of Drained?"

"We think it's spiritual."

We stopped at the corner meaning we were finally at the end of that hallway.

"The room is right there," he said pointing. I came up behind him and looked around the corner. "I'm going to get you to the door, scan my thumb and get you back inside."

"I'm pretty much screwed, aren't I?"

"Yes, but I give you a lot of credit for attempting an escape by yourself."

"So you never answered my question."

"Which one?" he asked looking at me, standing straight up.

"What are you? I mean you're not a Sayou?"

"I'm a Kanyou. Hurry."

He signaled me forward, quickly scanned his thumb, and opened the door.

"Thank you," I said walking into the room.

Penny swarmed me with a hug, and Petey was smiling, but was holding Mickey. I heard the door close with a quiet click.

"You okay?" Petey asked.

"I was able to get away. I think we have someone here who is willing to help us."

"Help us, get out?" Penny asked.

I walked closer to him and Mickey.

"Yes. He helped me get back here. My Sayou is somewhere still looking for me."

"Who helped you?"

"It's a Kanyou."

Chapter 8

The light has been on in our room for hours now, I'm sure. I was sitting with Mickey who has yet to wake up since before I left. I covered his face to block the light.

"I can't just sit here and wait for something else to happen. We all need to get out," Petey suggested.

"We can't carry Mickey. We should let him heal for a little while longer. I wouldn't mind a few hours longer of recover time. My turn will come again soon enough." I said.

I looked down at Mickey. He really did look peaceful, even though the situation was anything but.

The door burst open and my symbol was on his belt. He looked pretty upset.

"Don't play dumb. It will not work this time."

"Fine, you want to go. Let's go. It's not going to work though. I'm too smart for you guys."

The Sayou came in. He bent over until his eyes were even with mine.

"Any little mind trick you might play, will not work. We've had many kids try and fail with all different sorts of mind tricks. Each failed, most ended up *dead*."

My stomach flipped with his last word, but I didn't let it show on my face. I got up on my own accord, gently lifting Mickey's head. Penny came over and sat where I sat, and left the room with out one touch from the Sayou. I didn't turn around, because I trusted myself enough to come back to my friends. They trusted me to get them out. To get them home, and I can't let myself fail them.

I walked right up to the chairs and sat down allowing the wrist and ankle straps to restrain me. My Sayou stood in front of me and waited for me to lay my head back. I resisted at first, but then thought of Mickey. I laid back and felt the metal strap around my head.

Just relax. You can do this.

I took a deep breath and felt his finger on the strap. I saw my adventure from the mirror world. I saw dad, grandpa and my mom. I fought against what he was trying to extract from me. I gave him other memories besides that last one of my mom.

"No," I yelled. "It's mine and YOU, CAN'T, HAVE IT!"

Everything went black. My world went silent and dark.

φ φ φ

"Moni," I heard. I was still very much in a daze. I was trying to sit up and felt hands on my shoulders. "Lay down."

"Where am I?"

"You're safe. You're with us. Moni, it's Penny. Wake up. Come back to us. Petey and Mickey are waiting for you."

My vision became less blurry as my eyes focused on the light above me. I saw a black silhouette block the light from my view.

"Penny?"

"It's me. Open your eyes all the way hon. You can do it."

"It's done," I said.

"What's done?" I heard Petey ask.

"My Drain is done. Nothing happened. I think it killed him. I hurt him by not giving him what he wanted. What he needed."

I sat up with Penny's help.

"And that was your memory?" she asked.

"Yes. The Sayou said they heal because it's for their survival."

"That's right," Penny said putting her hand to her chin.

"I guess Mickey never got that message." Petey said looking down at Mickey.

The light in our room went off, and to my surprise so did the light under the floor. For once we were in an almost dark room. If it wasn't for the small lights in the fountain the three of us would be blind to what could be coming.

"Sleep," Petey suggested. "We all need it. If we do plan on getting out of here with or without the Kanyou we will need our strength."

Petey was right. I crawled next to Mickey and curled into the little body heat he still had. Petey put his red hoodie over Mickey's slightly shivering body. Petey got out from under Mickey and lay behind him. I cuddle closer to Mickey trying to keep him warm. Penny lay behind me the way she always did and the four of us had ourselves a power nap.

φ φ φ

"Let go of me," Petey yelled.

I was startled awake and was up on my feet in a matter of seconds. "Petey. Petey, listen to me. They are going to heal your arm."

Petey started fighting just to hear what I had to tell him.

"You are going to have to relax. Don't do what I did. It will make it that much harder the second time around. Let them heal the burn. You don't want that memory. The memory where you lost everything you had left of your parents."

He stopped struggling when those words slipped from my lips. I didn't mean it, but at the same time, I meant every word. Maybe they will take the memory with the scar. I turned to Penny. "The burn on his arm. It's not a scar. It happened two days ago. It's not healed yet. They can't heal something that isn't ready to be taken. His body is still in that process. It will do more harm than good."

I ran to the door, but it was slammed right in my face. I hit the door really hard with my fist. The bang of the metal vibrated throughout the room.

"Moni," Penny said.

I turned to look at her.

"Mickey is awake."

I quickly walked over to him and Penny. I looked down at him. "He looks pale."

"He's dehydrated."

I looked for the sleeve that Petey had had last night. It was still over in the spot where Petey slept a few minutes ago. I picked it up and went over to the fountain. I dipped the cloth in and squeezed out the excess. I put my hand underneath the cloth to not waste any of the water. I knelt down next to Mickey. He opened his mouth as I lowered the cloth then squeezed most of the water into his mouth.

"Better?"

"Better," he repeated.

I dropped the moist cloth next to me and sat down. I put my hand on Mickey's and looked at the strength starting to come back to him.

φ φ φ

We were sitting against the wall. Penny's head was on my shoulder and Mickey was lying on my lap. I was starring at the wall waiting for my closest friend to come back to me.

"What if he can't walk? What if he ends up like Mickey? How will we ever get out of here if that happens?"

"Moni, stop that."

"I can't. Not with all that we have gone through in these pass three months. I've been hyped up on negative thoughts and adrenaline ever since I saw my mom."

"You can't eliminate the positive side to things. There are still good things."

"Like what?" I asked rolling my eyes.

"Us," Mickey said.

I looked down to him and tears came to my eyes.

"I'm sorry," I said starting to break down. I was supposed to be the leader. The leader that would be strong and never show the true fear I had built up ever since the first world.

"Moni," Penny said lifting her head up to look at me. "It's okay to be scared."

"I'm terrified. I'm going to lose Petey."

"He's stronger than you think," she said putting her hand on my shoulder.

"I'm sure he is. You guys have trusted me for so long, and I go and bring you into this world. This world that might break us."

The door opened with a loud click. I quickly got up moving Mickey's head off my lap. I get myself to the door in time to catch Petey that was pushed in and can hardly stand. I gently put him down onto the floor and got over to the door before they had time to close it. I put my foot into the crack in the door and kept it from closing.

"Give me something to put in here!" I yelled.

I looked behind me and saw Penny jump up. She was looking around the room frantically trying to find something to replace my foot. She looked over to the fountain and I saw her grab one of the small statues. I guess it was cheap gold because with one swift bend I heard it snap off. She threw it over and I forced it into the gap. I removed my foot leaving the weight of the door on the small fragile gold design.

"It's not going to hold," I said.

Penny came up next to me. We started hearing the small cracks of something right before it breaks into a million little pieces.

"You tried," she said putting her hand on my shoulder. "We'll find a different way out."

"Where! Through the window," I said pointing to the window. "Duh."

Chapter 9

It felt so good to have all four of us in the room again. Petey was on my lap. I looked down at his arm that was still wrapped in gauze. My curiosity was getting the better of me. Penny went to get the cloth wet for him, and I started to unwrap his gauze. The burn was not healed. He found a way to fight. He might have killed his Sayou too.

"What are you smiling about? Are you seeing a positive side to all this?" Penny said giving me the cloth.

"Not really, but . . ." I stopped mid sentence and looked down so Penny could see.

"He did it," she smiled.

"You will be next. All you have to do is fight what they want to take, and we'll be home free."

"They are going to take my emotions. My tears, my laughter," she stated, and her smile dwindled away.

"Not if you fight the way you have been fighting. And not if we get out of here before then."

I felt Petey's head move, and looked down.

"Petey," I said touching his hair.

"What," he said in a tired voice.

"Are you okay?"

"I fought it. Just like you told me. I did it," he smiled.

"You still have your burn. You still have the memory?"

"It's the last memory I have of them. I would like to keep it, even if it hurts."

He started to sit up. He lifted his arm and looked at his burn. He gently traced it with his pointer finger. He could tell I was looking at him. I handed him the gauze back and he started wrapping it back up. I looked at the door remembering the statue I had put in the door. It was still there, and the door was still ajar.

"Let's get out of here," I said pointing to the door.

Everyone seemed to be in a little bit of shock that the small statue held open that big, heavy door.

"Can you get up?" I asked Petey who was just finishing up wrapping him arm.

"Yeah," he said slowly getting up. I steadied him when he was up.

"All right Mickey," I said. "It's your turn."

I went over to him and offered both my hands. He grabbed them. I pulled and Penny stood behind him to help me out. He was a little wobbly getting his balance, but seemed fine once we started for the door.

"The door won't stay open by itself. I'll pull the door open so you guys can get out, then I'll need one, or all of you to hold it while I slide through. It will be loud when it closes though, so we'll have to get to a dark place. Once they see an empty room, we'll be playing hide and seek until we run into the Kanyou, hopefully."

"And if we don't find the Kanyou, then what?" Mickey asked.

I paused. "We'll be screwed."

"That's cool," Petey said low and sarcastic.

"Are we ready?"

"Ready as ever," Petey said. He came over to me and gave me a small kiss. "Let's do this."

I faced the door and slowly started to pull it open. Petey grabbed with me and we both pulled. Mickey and Penny slide out.

"You go next," Petey suggested.

"No, you," I grunted.

"You," Petey argued.

"Fine."

I let go of the door, and already knew the door became so much heavier on Petey.

"Penny, help me," I asked quietly.

We grabbed the door the same way Petey and I had. He slipped through. I told Penny to let go and we ran to the same hallway that I met up with the Kanyou.

As we rounded the first corner I heard Sayous talking. Either they were bored or they just realized we weren't in our room anymore. I stopped and pushed everyone else toward the dark hallway. I slowly followed them and worked my way to the front grabbing hands on the way. I felt around and finally found the hallway. I tried to remember where to step over things in the hallways, but slid my feet across the floor to make it easier. I felt Penny's hand squeeze mine.

"Do we have everyone?" I asked quietly.

"I'm good," Petey answered.

"Good," Mickey said.

We continued forward until we got the end of the hallway. We are now across from the door, and the few Sayous that stood in front of it. I don't think they know we are gone yet. They would be freaking out if they knew. I was now waiting for an opening to get us away from here, but then a few more Sayous came to the door. I think they just found out. The door opened and I peeked around the corner. I think it was Penny's Sayou that walked in. They were expecting her to be there, but I had something different in mind. I saw that the remaining Sayous walked in after Penny's and I pulled my head back behind the wall. I then heard the door shut. I quickly looked around the corner, and to my eyes, the door was really shut. Was it him? Was he watching?

"What was that?" I heard Petey say a little frazzled.

"Something touched me too," Mickey said.

Something velvet touched my hand and I knew it was the Kanyou.

"Nice job," he said.

"Thanks. Now what?"

"I know of a portal, but it's on the other side of this Capsule."

"Capsule? How far is it?"

"That's what they call their home. It's a little bit of a hike, but it's the way back home."

"Why are you helping us?" Penny asked.

"It's our job."

"Our?"

"Let's go," he said leading the way out of the hallway. We took a different way into the Drain room. He led us the long way around our room. I guess he didn't want to risk the Sayous seeing us. "Hurry."

We ran across the giant Drain room. We were about half way when everything went dark and quiet. I ran into the Kanyou, not realizing he stopped. My friends then ran into me, knocking the Kanyou forward.

"Sssh," he said.

A bright flash definitely caught my attention to my left.

"Where do you think you are going? These are my Minds. You are not going to take anymore of them."

Chapter 10

I looked over to the bright light and saw a very tall and skinny shadow standing in front of it.

"Who's that?"

"Leader. He only comes out when Minds that have not been Drained try to leave."

I looked back at Penny. She has not been Drained yet. I thought she was going to get out of here with an easy pass. I was wrong. *Crap.* She let go of my hand and I turned around. She was backing up. She was slowly heading back the way we came. I looked to see the path from where we came and the Sayous closed us in. Penny was going to have to fight Leader and she was going to have to win. This might kill her.

I slowly drop back to where Penny was. The boys followed me. Kanyou had held his ground looking at the faces of nearly all the Sayou that surrounded us. I held Penny's hand the tightest I could and told myself to not let go. I felt that weird connection between her and I. It was the same feeling from that first world. I had somehow made a connection with her even though she was miles away from me strapped to a machine, on the brink of death. I don't know how I did it the first time, and its is happening again right now, but I don't think she could feel anything. Leader blinked in and out of my vision until something else completely took over my mind and my sight. I think I was seeing Penny's memory. I thought we weren't supposed to see each other's memories. It was like against the rules. I was somehow seeing what happened to her brother. I was seeing Penny in her living room. She was watching cartoons until I saw her mom come into the room. She turned the channel to the news. The vision zoomed into the back of her head in the foreground with a plane crash on the news in the background. I couldn't hear anything the news people were saying, if they were saying anything. I remembered her telling me about her brother coming home for the summer. He was away at college and decided to take a plane home, instead of the family traveling all the way to Oklahoma in a car. The plane he was on crashed due to turbulence.

I came out of her memory and Leader was standing in front of the four of us. Mickey, Petey and I stood in front of Penny. I saw Kanyou come over and stand between Leader and us. I held onto Kanyou's waistband, hoping Leader would change his mind about fighting and let us leave.

That would have been too easy. He one handedly threw Kanyou to the side with one hand. He took a step towards us and reached over us to grab Penny. He lifted her up around the waist and went toward the chairs. I looked over at Kanyou who got up without hesitation. I saw him take a small dagger out of nowhere. It extended into a long stick with the dagger tip on the end. He hit the leg of Leader and caught his attention. Leader stopped and flicked his wrist. Some of the Sayous that were around us went to Kanyou and encircled him. They grabbed Kanyou by his arms and dragged him to the chairs following Leader and Penny. The only thing I could do was watch.

I slowly followed Kanyou to the chairs and couldn't see anything because the Sayous had formed a circle in front of the chairs. Even if Penny could get out of the chair she would have no way of getting out of harm's way. *I can't just stand by and let this happen to her.* I pushed my way through feeling Sayous putting their hands on me. I kept pushing forward breaking every grasp they had put on me.

"Stop!" I yelled.

I felt like I was standing alone. I thought the boys would follow me. I looked behind me and there was nothing but Sayous.

"You will not interrupt," Leader said in a deep ugly voice.

"I already have."

He turned away from Penny and Kanyou and started toward me.

"I've already been Drained. You can't do anything to me."

"I *can* make you watch your friend die."

"Friend*s*," I said looking to Kanyou.

I felt Sayous surround me and walk forward. I had no choice but to walk with them.

"Where are Petey and Mickey?" Penny asked with tears in her eyes.

"I don't know."

I then remembered how I know what Penny's memory is.

"Pay close attention," Leader said to me.

I gave him the dirtiest look I could before he turned back to Penny. He stood up straight and slowly lifted his hand to the thumbprint on the metal headband. He closed his eyes and so did Penny. So did I.

I saw a plane crash into the dirt ground as if I was standing only a few miles from it. I felt the earth quake and felt the wind whip through the air. I could feel the dirt hit my skin and my knees collapse beneath me. The plane was nearly engulfed in flames as a small explosion echoed through the air. A puff of fire and smoke lifted into the sky and the crackle of the fires became too much to bear. I could feel my heart sink into my stomach and gravity take over. I fell to my knees and felt the hard ground under me. I kept my eyes on the plane and tears filled my eyes. I was now looking up at the white clouds that were being hidden by the black smoke of the crash. I could start to smell a hint of gasoline as I sat back on my feet trying to hold back tears. I tried to get my feet under me. I wanted to run as far away from this site as I could.

The trees rushed passed me until the path in front of me started to flicker through my teared, blurry vision.

No.

"Penny," I said in the softest voice I could muster.

"Moni, You can't be here."

"I was meant to be here. This is supposed to happen. Let me help."

"Don't let him take it," she prayed.

"Help me fight. Penny, this is your memory. Fight for it. Don't let him see your tears."

φ φ φ

I woke up with a headache and to a blinding light that started to overtake the giant room. I felt a hand helping me up, but it felt like velvet.

"How did you get out of the chair?"

"That's not important. We have to get you out of here."

"Why? I need to be here for her," I said sitting up with the help of his hand.

"She'll be fine. This light is the energy building up between them. We need to get somewhere safe."

"It won't hurt her. Will it?"

"If she can win, it won't hurt her," Kanyou said reassuring me.

I had so many questions to ask him, but I knew all he wanted was the boys and I safe. He got me to my feet and we ran passed the wall of Sayous to the boys. Mickey was in Petey's arms. He was out cold. He didn't know we were in trouble. Kanyou let go of me and ran to the boys. He picked Mickey up and I grabbed Petey's hand. We went to our room that was now empty. All the Sayous must have been called to the Drain room. Kanyou pushed us in and closed the door behind us. I went over to the window and could see the Drain room and chairs. The light seemed a little more bearable to look at behind the window. All there was left to do now was wait, and hope that she did it. That she pulled through like she did with everything else. Hopefully I did my fair share of helping her.

Chapter 11

I was sitting at the window when the light started to die down. I was looking at the floor with Mickey on my lap. Kanyou was standing by the door ready to defend us if he needed to, and Petey was no more than two feet from me leaning against the base of the water fountain. The water was no longer running and the small lights were also off.

"Do you think she did it?" Petey asked.

"I'm sure she did," I said low with a small spark of hope.

I heard the door open and jumped to the sound of it. Kanyou left, closing the door behind us. I kept my eye on him the whole time. He was going out into the Drain room. Everything in that room was still. He knelt down and gently picked up a small black shadow.

Penny.

I slowly got out from under Mickey's body and stood by the door twirling my thumbs. I heard the soft steps of Kanyou. He creaked the door open just enough so him and Penny could slip through, then closed it again behind him. He brought Penny to the middle of the room and lightly placed her on the water floor. I put my hand to her face, then to her neck, hoping to feel a pulse. I could feel it. I could feel the life in her. She did it. She beat him, and now I get this feeling that this world will start crashing down around us, but nothing was happening. Nothing except quiet healing in this one peaceful room in this god forsaken world.

The four of us were now huddled by the fountain. Kanyou was crouching in front of us with his hand on Penny's head. Penny moved her head and opened her eyes to look up at me. Kanyou took his hand away, but I grabbed it to put it on her shoulder. Penny moved her head to look at the object that was now touching her. She smiled when she saw it was a hand. She touched it with the hand that was not holding mine and looked to Kanyou.

"Thank you," she said weakly.

"You should be thanking her," Kanyou said looking at me.

Penny turned her head back to me. "You shouldn't have done that. You could have gotten hurt."

"I could have gotten hurt in the machine world going after you because you saved me in the first place."

"True," she smiled.

Kanyou moved over to Mickey who was a few feet from me. He placed his hand on Mickey's head. Mickey moved his head to face Kanyou, and then opened his eyes.

"Let's get you guys home. You will need time to recover before moving onto what ever life has in store for you tomorrow."

"Why did you help us?"

"It has been our job since the beginning of time to end this ritual the Sayous have, and we did. With the help of four brave humans, we did it."

"Who's we?" I asked.

"My clan."

The metal door to our room squeaked open and more faces that looked like Kanyou were now standing in the doorway.

"Oh."

φ φ φ

An endless line of Kanyous came in, slowly and peacefully. A few came over to Penny, and me, some went to Mickey and Petey, and the others stood by the door.

"How are we getting home? The portal dropped us here when we entered," I asked pointing to the ceiling of our room.

"Just follow her," Kanyou said pointing to an older clan member.

"Who is she?" Penny asked.

"She knows where all the portals are and where they lead."

"That's cool," I said looking to Penny.

Kanyou left and blended into to his matching clan. *How do they know who's who?*

"Don't be afraid," the Kanyou said to me. "My name is Kayo."

"You all have names?" Penny asked.

"Who was the Kanyou who helped us?" I asked right after Penny.

"His name is Kanyou. He has show the true being of what a Kanyou is. He doesn't need a name."

Kayo picked me up. He too felt like velvet, but I could see a slight difference in his skin color from Kanyou. Kayo's skin was bluer, while Kanyou was more gray blue. Penny and her Kanyou were behind us. I guessed Mickey and Petey were up a few Kanyous.

I was able to lay my head against Kayo's body. He was so unbelievably smooth, and oddly warm.

"Rest," he said.

I wanted to, but I needed to make sure the four of us got home.

I relaxed my head on his chest and arm. I couldn't help but relax with the motion of his walk, and the smoothness of his skin. I closed my eyes and sleep took over instantly.

φ   φ   φ

My black dreamless sleep became full of water reflections on the black walls. I felt like I was going mock three through nowhere.

I woke up on grass near the water's edge. My hand over hung the grass' border and my fingertips were in the water. I quickly took my hand out and touched my fingers. They were wet, and cold. I was back in the real world. The world that I know I belong. The world where water was wet if you touched it.

I sat up and saw Penny near my feet, Mickey next to her, and looked next to me. Petey's hand was touching mine. I scooted closer to him and touched his cheek.

"Petey," I said. "We are home."

I realized that the sky was still dark. Were we not gone for long, or has it been a week and it is now night once again.

"Moni, you okay?"

I looked down to Penny. She was starting to sit up.

"We are home," she smiled.

"We did it."

"Moni," Petey said.

I looked down to him and gently kissed him.

"You okay?" I asked.

"Better now after that kiss."

"Haha," I said with a smile.

I looked over to Mickey, and then crawled over to him. "Mickey?"

"Wake up Mickey," Penny said.

I put my two fingers to his neck. There was a pulse.

"Let's get home." I looked back to Petey. "Can you carry him?"

"Be happy too."

"That, uh, that won't be necessary," Mickey said with his eyes still closed.

"How you feeling?" I asked.

"Like I got hit by a bus."

"I think we all feel like that," I said with a smile.

I stood up and held a hand down to him. Penny did the same. We pulled him up and put his arms around our shoulders. "Just until we get to the fence."

"I'm not going to argue."

His feet were barely helping, but they were better then having him as dead weight.

We finally got to my house, that was thankfully the second closest. Mickey's house was locked when we got there. His was the closest. Mine was only another two blocks.

We got Mickey up into my room and sat him on the day bed under my window. *Wait? I don't have a day bed?* I smiled and knew who had bought it for me.

Mickey lay down without a pillow or nothing. Petey fell onto the bed face first into the pillows. Penny plopped on the beanbag chair in the corner of my room near the closet. I went to close my door and I grabbed a few blankets and pillows out of the chest that was at the foot of my bed. I lay one over Mickey, and gently started to shove a pillow under his head until he lifted his head for me.

"Thank you," he said without opening his eyes.

"You're welcome," I said lightly kissing his head.

I lay a blanket over Penny who looked pretty comfortable without a pillow then lay down on the bed next to Petey. He had turned onto his back with one arm out inviting me to lay with him. His other hand was on his chest. I put my head on his shoulder waiting for him to hug me closer but he was out. I sat up and pulled my crocheted blanket over both of us.

I felt tears starting to sting my eyes. All my fear that was cooped up inside me during that whole adventure was coming out right now. I had to keep my crying low, but couldn't do anything about the tears getting Petey's shirt wet. It's not like he would feel it anyway. I was looking to my window, and kept glancing down to

Mickey. He was lucky. I could have lost him. *I just hope that luck will remain with us when the next world reveals itself. Hopefully it will show up later, rather than sooner.*

The adventures continue

Apart from Our

Own
Time

www.ingramcontent.com/pod-product-compliance
Lightning Source LLC
Chambersburg PA
CBHW050907120626
46554CB00003B/1051